the Test

contents

written by Glynne MacLean

illustrated by Serena Kearn

5 SCROLLS

PREDICT: In what time period and location do you think this story is set? What helped you form your opinion?

Today was the day. The day of the test. Janita bit her lip. If only she knew what it would involve. Why didn't anyone else look nervous? Did they know something she didn't?

Zac and Kain were hanging out of one of the fifth-floor windows, yakking to a mud mason repairing the exterior wall. Even Philippa looked unconcerned. She must know something. Philippa researched everything. Janita couldn't count the number of times she'd had to drag Philippa away from revising her studies a third or fourth time.

Janita was about to catch her arm when the adjudicator swept in. Without a word, he laid out five scrolls on the central floor tile.

Janita nudged Philippa in the ribs. "Why five?" she asked. "There are only four ot us."

The adjudicator's glare silenced Philippa's response and dragged the boys in from the window.

"The test commences from the moment the critical scroll is opened," the adjudicator announced.

"That's the one that determines who takes the test," Philippa murmured to Janita.

"Correct," agreed the adjudicator. The critical scroll is blank. The other four are not.

"But what is the test?" Janita asked.

CLARIFY:
mud mason
adjudicator
scrolls
collective actions
apprenticeships

2

ANALYSE: Why do you think the adjudicator introduced the threat of banishment to the wilderness? What effect did he want his warning to have on the contestants? Why?

The nature of the Survival Test and the outcome will be determined by your collective actions. Fail and you will all be banished to the wilderness. Pass and you will commence your apprenticeships.

With a swirl of his tunic, the adjudicator departed.

For a second, no one moved, then Kain sprang forward and grabbed all five scrolls. He held them high above his head and danced around the room. "What am I bid? The highest bidder gets the critical scroll."

"Don't be daft," Philippa said to her brother. "You don't know which is which."

"Then I'll open them all," Kain said. He dropped down onto his haunches, tucking them between his feet. Before he could unfurl one, Zac gave him a shove, toppling him over and scattering the scrolls.

Philippa, Zac and Kain pounced, snaffling one each. Janita was left staring at two identical scrolls. She knew she had to pick one – but which?

AUTHOR PURPOSE: Why do you think the author does not give any details about the apprenticeships?

she knew she had to pick one – but which?

3

"Aww, what?" snorted Kain, staring at his opened scroll. "Nothing but a lousy number five. What a rip-off!"

"I've got a four on mine," said Zac. "Let's open another."

"You can't," said Philippa. **You've already opened one. Look at your fingers.**

Zac's eyes widened as he saw the ten fluorescent fours pulsating back at him from his fingertips. "Magic," he breathed.

"What have you got, Philippa?" Janita asked.

"A three."

4

you have to choose...

CLARIFY:
fluorescent
pulsating
emblazoned
dithering

"So the blank one is one of those," said Kain. He jabbed a finger, emblazoned with the digit five, at the remaining scrolls. "Go on, Janita. Choose!"

"But..." Janita began.

"But nothing," Kain snapped. "Just pick one – either one will do. Stop dithering. Just pick one."

Janita stared from one scroll to the other.

She didn't want to take the test.

"But what if mine's not blank? What then? Who'll take the test?"

They all looked at Philippa, but she shrugged. "Janita," she said, "you have to choose."

Janita's stomach tightened.

"Pick that one!" said Zac.

"No, this one," said Kain.

"Be quiet," Philippa commanded. "It must be Janita's decision."

"But..." Janita began again.

"Get on with it," Zac said. "At this rate the monsoons will have come and gone before you decide."

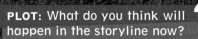

PLOT: What do you think will happen in the storyline now?

Riddle

"Okay, okay. This one." Janita pointed to the least crumpled scroll, but made no move towards it.

"Okay, that's it," said Kain. "Give it here."

"No," Janita said, snatching it up. "It's my scroll. I'll open it." She ignored Kain, who was mouthing imitations of her at Zac as she split the seal. Her heart sank.

It was blank.

She had to take the test.

Before anyone could say anything, the adjudicator flung open the door. He turned to Janita. "Will you swim, descend or surf?" he demanded.

The scroll dropped from her fingers as she stammered, "Um, I ah... can't swim."

Raising his voice, he bellowed, "Swim, descend or surf?"

"She'll descend," Zac said. "Won't you, Janita?" Janita nodded.

"You will be escorted beyond the World-end Gates," said the adjudicator.

Into the wilds? breathed Kain.

VISUAL FEATURES:
What messages do the design and visual images on this page send to the reader? How do these messages enhance your interpretation of the story?

OPINION: Do you think the author stereotypes Zac and Kain? Why/why not?

will you swim, descend or surf?

The adjudicator swept on. "It is up to the others to guide you back." He stabbed a finger towards the door. "Now go!"

Zac grabbed Janita's scroll and thrust it at her. "You'll need this. It's magic."

The last thing they saw was Janita's terrified face as the guards escorted her away.

The adjudicator's final words clattered into the silence like rocks into a chasm.

" Look to your scrolls. Solve the riddle and guide her home.

LANGUAGE FEATURE:
Simile/Metaphor/
Personification:
What literary device has the author used here? What was the purpose for using this device?

ANALYSE: What inferences can you make about the words/actions of the adjudicator? What effect do you think the adjudicator was hoping to have on the contestants?

Zac barely noticed him depart. His eyes were fixed on his scroll. The number four had vanished. In its place were words that read: **" In darkness – walls below support walls above. "**

"Aww, what?" muttered Kain. "I hate riddles."

"What does yours say?" Philippa asked him.

Kain rolled his eyes. "Unity shines bright and scrolls do speak," he read slowly.

"So we have to work together," Zac said. "We write on our scrolls and, if we agree, Janita will see it."

"How do you know that?" Philippa and Kain asked together.

Zac shrugged. "That's what the message on your scroll says. It's obvious. Not like mine. I've no idea what mine means."

"Or mine," Philippa said. "Let's put them in numerical order. My number was three, Zac's was four and Kain's five. Maybe that'll help."

They laid each scroll out in order and read:

"At sight of bleeding dragon's lair descend
In darkness — walls below support walls above
Unity shines bright and scrolls do speak."

The three exchanged glances, but no one wanted to admit they were flummoxed.

"We need a map," Philippa said at last.

"Nah," yelled Kain, dashing to the door. "The roof. From there we'll be able to see everything. You know – where they've taken her. Come on."

INFERENCE: What inferences can you make about the society the four contestants live in, based on their response to authority?

CLARIFY:
numerical
lair
flummoxed

unity shines and bright scrolls do speak

Unity shines bright and scrolls do speak

In darkness - walls below support walls above

At sight of Unveiling dragon's lair ascend

JANITA   KAIN   ZAC   PHILIPPA

CHARACTER ANALYSIS: What do you know about the characters so far from textual and inferential information?

Up on the baking roof, they turned their backs on the array of sailing ships in the harbour and the smaller vessels moored along the tidal head of Gigantem River. Instead, they looked to the uninhabited wilds beyond the protective town walls, beyond the World-end Gates.

CLARIFY:
array
opaque
frankincense trees
simultaneously

Kain peered through the opaque haze that hung above the sand and bristled about the trunks of the scattered frankincense trees. At first he could see nothing. He shaded his eyes from the scornful glare of the sun, trying not to squint.

Now he could see a wavy smudge in motion.

Over there, he yelled, pointing towards the mountains.

"Two camels," Philippa said, peering in the direction of his finger. "I can't tell how many people or which way they're going. Do you think it's her?"

"Who else?" asked Kain. "They're too far inland to be frankincense tappers, since the trees are all coastal. The dragon's blood tappers work in the mountains, but they never travel in twos."

INFERENCE:
What inferences can you make about the name World-end Gates?

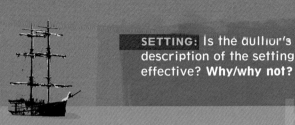

SETTING: Is the author's description of the setting effective? **Why/why not?**

...beyond the world-end gates

"That's it! Kain, you're a genius," exclaimed Philippa.

Kain swaggered a little as his sister explained her excitement. "The dragon's blood trees grow up there." She pointed to the mountain range.

LANGUAGE FEATURE:

Simile/Metaphor/ Personification: What literary device has the author used here? How did it help your understanding?

The bleeding dragon's lair, Zac murmured, remembering the words on Philippa's scroll.

"Exactly!" Philippa said.

"So, Janita has to descend when she first sees the mountain?" asked Kain slowly.

"No, when she first sees the gullies where the trees grow," Zac said. He unfurled his scroll and looked at each of them in turn. "Do we all agree on that?"

At their nods, he began tracing a message with his forefinger on the scroll. Sure enough, the words began to appear without any ink. All he could hope was that they were appearing simultaneously on Janita's scroll.

ISSUE: What issues could arise from the way the test is set up? What is your stance on these issues?

DESCENT

Janita couldn't believe it. She'd dismounted as instructed and taken the sack handed to her. Then, as she stooped to put it down, the guardswoman had wheeled the camels and wandered off.

Janita stared after them, then gulped and wiped her gritty eyes. Her mind screamed, "Don't leave me!" But she knew that to shout or scream was a waste of energy. In the desert, conserve energy. That's what they'd been taught. Easy to say in a classroom, but out here, in the heat and burning sand...

QUESTION:
"Immobility was benign."
What does this mean?

A forked tongue flickered in her peripheral vision. A snake smelling the air. Janita rolled her eyes sideways to see it more clearly. She had to stay still. Immobility was benign, the scholar had said. Her knees mustn't shake.

Movement meant threat.

For an age, the striped snake sniffed. At last, it dropped to the ground and, whipping sideways, departed.

Janita exhaled, her knees folding under her. But, the instant she touched the blistering sand, she shot upright again, stifling a howl. She mustn't cry. She couldn't afford to lose moisture. "Think," she told herself, repeating it over and over until the pounding in her chest calmed.

CLARIFY:
peripheral vision
benign

12

don't leave
me...

LANGUAGE FEATURE:

"A snake smelling the air."
"Movement meant threat."
"The sack!"
"Nothing else. No map.
No instructions. Nothing."
Why does the author use short sentences in this section of the story? What effect does this have?

The sack! Supplies, thought Janita. Inside, she found her scroll, an oil lamp – unlit but full of oil – and a goatskin of water. Nothing else. No map. No instructions. Nothing. What now? She looked up. She was alone. Alone, that is, except for the snakes and scorpions...

BEYOND THE TEXT: How do you think Janita's survival training will help her in the desert?

What real-world connections can you make?

LANGUAGE FEATURE:
Alliteration – the repetition of consonant sounds to achieve emphasis or convey mood or emotion. **Can you find any?**

She clapped a hand over her mouth. She mustn't imagine the worst. Must think positively. The test had to be passable – somehow.

Zac had thought the scroll was magical. Would that help? She unfurled it and stared. What before had been blank papyrus now read:

"At first sight of the gullies where the dragon's blood trees grow, you'll find a cave entrance. That's where you descend."

Janita's mind grasped at the word "cave" and furnished it with bats, dead ends, darkness and a myriad of creepy-crawlies. It took a moment for her common sense to counter with the alternative – searing sun, snakes, scorpions and dehydration.

Janita shouldered the sack and turned to face the mountains. Yes, she could see the outline of the gullies. She looked left, then right, then spotted what must be the cave entrance.

An outcrop of rock, with a black opening at its centre.

Soon after, hot and panting from the short climb, Janita found herself hesitating at the cave entrance. She reread the scroll, squared her shoulders, and began to pick her way down into it.

Again she wavered. As her eyes adjusted, she could see a wide passage leading back in the direction of the town. It was lit by minute cracks in the white, room-high cave ceiling. Beneath each crack lay a small deposit of sand. Janita focused her eyes on each successive deposit, which lay a metre or two apart, and began walking.

SETTING:

Analyse the elements that helped you form an impression of the cave system. What mood or feelings are evoked by the author's description?

hoping against hope...

Four more steps in and a weird clicking noise filled the air. At the sixth mound, Janita was enveloped by a nauseating smell. It was disgusting – like putrid fish drenched in urine.

Now something squelched underfoot. Bat dung! Janita covered her nose and accelerated. Deeper into the cave, the stench dissipated. Just as Janita was deciding that maybe the test wasn't too bad after all, the cracks in the ceiling disappeared.

PERSONAL RESPONSE:
How did you connect to Janita's feelings as she faced her fears underground? How would you react if you were placed in the same situation?

Ahead it was pitch black.

Janita scrabbled in the sack for the lamp, then remembered there was nothing to ignite it with. Deflated, she sat down carefully and leant her back against the cool rock wall. As she fished out the goatskin for a drink, she saw that the scroll was emitting a soft glow. Hoping against hope, she unrolled it and read: "What's happening?"

SYMBOLISM:
"...the scroll was emitting a soft glow."
Do you think there is also a symbolic meaning contained in this reference?
Why/why not?

What's happening?

WALLS ABOVE AND WALLS BELOW

"Why hasn't she answered?" Philippa asked. "Do you think she's okay?"

Kain rolled his eyes. "Stress not! Do something useful. Sort out the riddle."

"There's no point in working it out if she's dead somewhere," snapped Philippa.

CLARIFY:
bickering
perplexed
navigable

Zac raised his hands. **" We have to work together, remember?**

Bickering isn't going to help Janita or us. She's in a cave, right? So the walls below could be the cave walls, couldn't they?"

Philippa's eyes lit up. "Ifri – that's an ancient word for cave, isn't it?"

Kain twirled a finger near his ear. Zac nodded, perplexed.

"The Ifri district," continued Philippa. "You know – the invasions?"

"No," said Zac and Kain together, shaking their heads.

"During the invasions, our ancestors hid in the caves under the town," explained Philippa. "It's a cross-faulted cave system, so two sets of parallel passages go at right angles to each other. Most are dead ends. They built the roads above to match the navigable passages below. That way, they could memorise the layout and navigate the caves without light, if necessary."

you don't get it...

SETTING: How credible is the description of the underground cave system? What details, in your opinion, made the setting believable/unbelievable?

"So?" asked Kain.

Philippa heaved a sigh. "You don't get it, do you?"

"Oh, I get it!" snapped Kain. "It's you who doesn't get it."

"Get what?" Philippa was yelling now.

A map's no good, Kain yelled back, if you don't know where you are! And we don't know where Janita is.

Zac thought about telling them not to argue, then thought better of it. He squabbled with his sister all the time. Instead, he unrolled his scroll and wrote to Janita, explaining how to write back to them via her scroll.

Janita hadn't had a chance to respond when Philippa stormed off.

INFERENCE What inferences can you make about Zac's decision not to interfere in the argument between Kain and Philippa? Do you think he should have intervened? **Why/why not?**

17

"Don't look at me," said Kain with a smirk.

Zac shook his head and rolled up his scroll.

"Yeah, yeah," said Kain. "If we don't cooperate, we all lose. I know."

They caught up with a puffy-eyed Philippa halfway through town. Zac kicked Kain in the shins, warning him not to tease her, and together the three of them threaded their way through narrow streets with multi-storey buildings on either side, dodging camels, kids, street vendors and potholes.

As they entered the Ifri district, the pattern of the streets changed. Instead of winding back and forth like wriggling snakes, the constricted Ifri streets intersected at right angles.

Philippa stopped, sniffed and rubbed her eyes. The boys ground to a halt, too. No one spoke.

Zac shot a look at his scroll. Janita still hadn't answered.

What if Philippa was right?

What if something had happened to her?

What then?

Kain slapped his forehead. "Duh! Man, I'm dumb."

Philippa and Zac exchanged nods, both stifling giggles.

"The town wall," continued Kain, ignoring them, "It's obvious. She must be heading back towards the town. So we should start at the wall and work in..."

"To where?" Philippa asked.

"Ah," said Kain. "Good question."

"What about a well?" suggested Zac. "She's underground..."

"I told you I was brilliant," interrupted Kain. "Come on. The Ifri well is this way. All we have to do is find the route from the wall to the well."

" And somehow convince Janita,

Zac muttered under his breath.

if we don't cooperate, we all lose...

QUESTION GENERATE:

What questions could you ask about the origin of the town and the wilderness surrounding it?

OPINION: Do you think the author has stereotyped Philippa? Why/why not?

Janita sat hunched in the scroll's pool of dim light. The response to her written description of her whereabouts had been one word: "Wait."

For what? Janita wondered. She kept hearing weird scuttling noises and the distant, bass calls of giant geckos. Worse still, her legs felt like a parade ground for a million marching critters.

Janita leapt to her feet and started jumping up and down on the spot. Anything to stop things crawling over her.

Just for a moment, she thought she saw a light glowing somewhere up ahead.

Then nothing.

CLARIFY:
intermittent
pitch-black darkness
discernible

Janita stood still. Had she imagined it, like the bugs? No, there it was again – and again. Was it coming towards her? It was too faint to tell. No, it *was* coming towards her! But, instead of brightening, the intermittent light faded away.

Then, just as Janita's legs began to itch again, glowing footprints appeared above her head.

Janita grabbed the scroll and wrote, "I can see footprints on the ceiling. Is that you?"

Within a split second, her words were replaced with, "Yes! Follow!"

With the sack over her shoulder, an arm outstretched and her eyes on the ceiling, Janita followed. She was enclosed in darkness, broken only by the shifting spotlight of footprints above.

Twenty paces in, they turned sharp left. The next turn was to the right, then a while later another right. Janita picked her way straight on for five minutes until, without warning, the footprints dimmed then vanished.

Stranded in pitch-black darkness, Janita froze. Just as she remembered the scroll, she again saw footprints ahead – dim but discernible. There were two sets going in different directions!

"What?" bellowed Janita.
The cave sent back an answer:
"What? What? What?"

what? what? what? what?

An echo, Janita told herself. It's just an echo.
Calm down.

She looked up. The illuminated footprints were
heading back towards her. As they met above her
head, they brightened and took a turn to the left.

Janita hesitated, then followed. As the texture
of the cave floor changed, they turned left
again. Now it was no longer gritty and dry
underfoot and Janita's sandals began to slip
and slide, almost toppling her to the ground.

CLARIFY:
confines
bisected

She didn't dare stop and ask
them to slow down.

Instead of reaching a hand into the darkness ahead,
she patted her way along the adjacent rock wall. It
helped her balance.

Janita's feet were beginning to ache by the time the
footprints turned right once more. For what seemed
an age, they went straight, then right again, followed
by another right into a passage barely wide enough
for Janita to squeeze through.

She tucked her elbows in and winced as cold water
sloshed around her ankles. The proximity of the damp
walls removed all fear of falling.

As the footsteps turned left, Janita felt a blast of warm
air. Here the water was up around her shins, but she
didn't care. Up ahead, there was light!
Not magic light, cast from scrolls
or footfalls, but real light.
Sunlight!

She could hear the faint calls of street vendors. She was
back within the town walls, underneath the streets.

With her eyes fixed on the sunshine, Janita splashed on as
fast as she could until she collided with a chest-high brick
wall. Within its confines, water sparkled in the sunlight.

A well, Janita thought. She looked around for a way out.
There were no steps and no way over the wall. She looked
up and saw a circle of blue sky bisected by a bar of
darkness. Then three familiar faces interrupted the smooth
curve of the well opening.

Three voices called, "Janita? Are you down there?"

It was Kain, Philippa and Zac.

QUESTION: How might the story have been different if Philippa had opened the critical scroll?

?

it's just an echo...echo...

BEYOND THE TEXT: What elements do you think help shift the setting of the underworld into a fantastical environment?

ASCENT

Kain punched a fist into the air then grabbed the large bucket propped up against the well.

"Get the donkey, Zac," he called.

Zac ran a hand up the well donkey's bristly back. He stepped in close to its flank so that, even if startled, it couldn't kick him. "Got it," Zac said quietly as he caught the bridle.

Kain heaved the bucket over the side of the well. It swung there, thumping from one side of the shaft to the other, until he and Philippa managed to stabilise it.

"Janita," Philippa called. "We're going to slowly lower the bucket for you to climb into. Stand back."

At Zac's nod, Kain released the well's wooden brake pin. Zac flicked the donkey's haunches and began leading it around the well. With each step, the roller, ropes and ratchet groaned, protesting at being disturbed. Philippa hung over the well lip, monitoring the bucket's descent.

"Stop," Philippa yelled, as Janita's muffled voice floated up to them. Zac stopped the donkey and held it stationary while Kain inserted the brake pin.

As Kain and Philippa tried to coax Janita into the bucket below, Zac unhitched the donkey, turned it about, and rehitched it. A frightened "no" could be heard wafting up the well shaft in response to every instruction Kain or Philippa called down.

At last, Kain snorted, "Yours," and flopped down in the shade of the well, muttering about drama queens.

We can't give up now,

hissed Philippa. She leaned back over the lip. "We won't drop you – I promise. Please don't cry. We're so close. You can do it, Janita."

BEYOND THE TEXT: What connections can you make to Janita's reluctance to trust the others and use the bucket for the rescue?

RESEARCH: How feasible do you think the technology described here is, based on technology trends to date?

CLARIFY: stabilise ratchet

PLOT: Has the plot been convincing/ unconvincing in your opinion? **Why?**

Zac rewarded the donkey with a handful of straw. They were getting nowhere fast. He scratched his head and looked about him. Beyond the crowd they had attracted, Zac spotted the unmistakable silhouette of the adjudicator, watching proceedings from a house opposite.

Zac tapped Philippa on the shoulder. "What exactly's the problem?"

"She says she can't climb over the wall into the well shaft and, even if she could, the ropes won't take her weight."

"Yeah, yeah, yeah," muttered Kain.

Zac dropped down onto his haunches and unfurled his scroll. He drew a diagram of the well, the donkey, the wooden gears, ratchets and handle. Beneath, he added an explanation of how the one-way ratchet system prevented the bucket from slipping.

what exactly's the
problem?

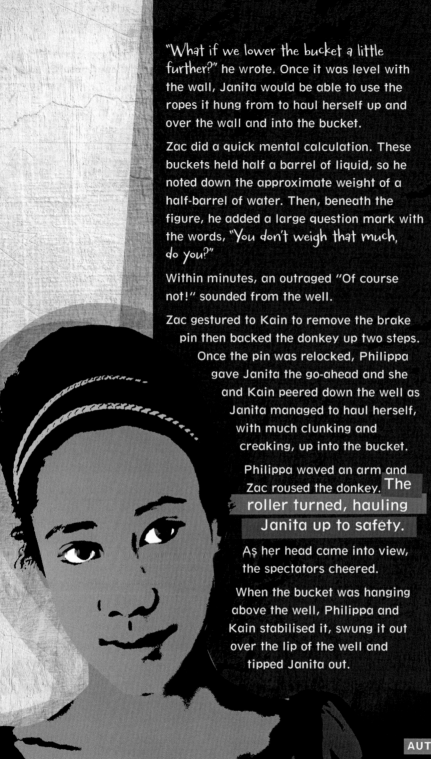

"What if we lower the bucket a little further?" he wrote. Once it was level with the wall, Janita would be able to use the ropes it hung from to haul herself up and over the wall and into the bucket.

Zac did a quick mental calculation. These buckets held half a barrel of liquid, so he noted down the approximate weight of a half-barrel of water. Then, beneath the figure, he added a large question mark with the words, "You don't weigh that much, do you?"

Within minutes, an outraged "Of course not!" sounded from the well.

Zac gestured to Kain to remove the brake pin then backed the donkey up two steps. Once the pin was relocked, Philippa gave Janita the go-ahead and she and Kain peered down the well as Janita managed to haul herself, with much clunking and creaking, up into the bucket.

Philippa waved an arm and Zac roused the donkey. The roller turned, hauling Janita up to safety.

As her head came into view, the spectators cheered.

When the bucket was hanging above the well, Philippa and Kain stabilised it, swung it out over the lip of the well and tipped Janita out.

CLARIFY:
disorderly heap

AUTHOR PURPOSE:
What messages do you think the author wanted to convey to the reader?

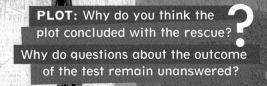

PLOT: Why do you think the plot concluded with the rescue?

Why do questions about the outcome of the test remain unanswered?

...into the piercing eyes of the adjudicator

She landed in a disorderly heap and they dusted her off while the crowd quietened, as if captured by a predator's gaze.

Zac looked up – straight into the piercing eyes of the adjudicator.

Hurriedly, the four stood to attention.

"Well done," said the adjudicator. "You commence your apprenticeships an hour after sun-up tomorrow."

And, with a swirl of his tunic, he departed, leaving them to celebrate.

They'd done it!
They had passed.

BEYOND THE TEXT: What do you think the apprenticeships will entail in this fantasy society?

27

Think about the Text

Making Connections

What connections can you make to the characters, plot, setting and themes of *The Test*?

Having hope

Feeling intimidated

Being afraid of failure

Losing confidence in yourself

Succeeding in something

text to

self

Recognising the importance of friendship

Facing adversity

Feeling abandoned

Being part of a team

text to text/**media**

**Talk about texts/media
you have read, listened to
or seen that have similar
themes and compare the
treatment of theme and the
differing author styles.**

text to **world**

**Talk about situations
in the world that might
connect to elements in
the story.**

Planning a
FANTASY story

Think about what
defines fantasy

Fantasy stories feature imaginary worlds
and magical or supernatural events.
The reader is called on to believe and accept
an alternative version of reality.

Think about the plot

Fantasy stories include action that depends on
real-world problems or conflict that are solved in a
fantastical/magical way.

Climax

Build your story to a
turning point. This is the
most exciting/suspenseful
part of the story.

Decide on an event
to draw the reader
into your story.
What will the main
conflict/problem be?

Conflict

Rising Action

Falling Action

Decide on a final
event that will
resolve the conflict/
problem and bring
your story to a close.

Set the scene:
who is the story
about? When and
where is it set?

Introduction

Resolution

Think about the characters

Explore:

- how they perceive their world

- how they respond to these fantastic places, events, time periods...

- how they think, feel and act and what motivates their behaviour

- the social structures of the imaginary community and how they affect the characters' status, appearance and behaviour.

Decide on the setting

Atmosphere/mood   **location**   **time**

Remember: Setting is an important part of creating a successful fantasy story. The identifying traits of fantasy are the inclusion of fantastic elements that may be hidden in or leak into an apparently real-world setting. The fantastical world should expand the reader's horizon and should be developed in detail to support the storyline.

Writing a FANTASY

Have you...

- dealt with real-world problems and solved them in a fantastical/magical way?

- used limited explanations for strange behaviours/events/objects?

- provided a window into another reality and possibility?

- explored social laws, values and beliefs of a different/extraordinary time and place?

- developed events that could be credible?

- used the setting to transport the reader to an imaginary world?

- used elements of science/physics principles to "dress up" the fantasy content?

- included elements/characters with special powers?

- created a consistent/logical story despite elements of magic and the supernatural?

...don't forget to revisit your writing. Do you need to change, add or delete anything to improve your story?